작은 암탉과 밀낟알갱이

The Little Red Hen and the Grains of Wheat

D1089832

Retold by L.R.Hen

Illustrated by Jago

Mantra Lingua

어느날 작은 암탉이 농지을 거닐다 밀 낟알갱이들을 주웠습니다.
"난 이 낟알들을 심을거야," 암탉은 생각했습니다.
"그러려면 도와줄 친구들이 필요해."

One day Little Red Hen was walking across the farmyard when she found
some grains of wheat.
"I can plant this wheat," she thought. "But I'm going to need some help."

작은 암탉이 농장 동물친구들에게 물었습니다.
"누구 낱알 심는걸 도와 주실래요?"
"난 안돼," 고양이가 말했습니다, "난 너무 바쁘거든."
"난 안돼," 개가 말했습니다, "난 너무 바쁘거든."
"난 안돼," 거위가 말했습니다, "난 너무 바쁘거든."

Little Red Hen called out to the other animals on the farm:
"Will anyone help me plant this wheat?"
"Not I," said the cat, "I'm too busy."
"Not I," said the dog, "I'm too busy."
"Not I," said the goose, "I'm too busy."

"그럼 나 혼자 심어야겠군," 암탉이 말했습니다.
암탉은 낟알들을 모두 심었습니다.

"Then I shall do it all by myself," said Little Red Hen.
She took the grains of wheat and planted them.

얼마간 비도 내리고 햇빛도 쪄 주었습니다.
낱알들은 무럭무럭 자라 금빛초원을 이루었습니다.
어느날 암탉은 낱알들이 다 자라 밀이 된 것을 보았습니다.
이제 밀들을 자를때가 되었읍니다.

The clouds rained and the sun shone. The wheat grew strong and tall and golden.
One day Little Red Hen saw that the wheat was ripe. Now it was ready to cut.

작은 암탉이 동물친구들에게 물었습니다.
"누구 밀 자르는걸 도와주실래요?"
"난 안돼," 고양이가 말했습니다, "난 너무 바쁘거든."
"난 안돼," 개가 말했습니다, "난 너무 바쁘거든."
"난 안돼," 거위가 말했습니다, "난 너무 바쁘거든."

Little Red Hen called out to the other animals:
"Will anyone help me cut the wheat?"
"Not I," said the cat, "I'm too busy."
"Not I," said the dog, "I'm too busy."
"Not I," said the goose, "I'm too busy."

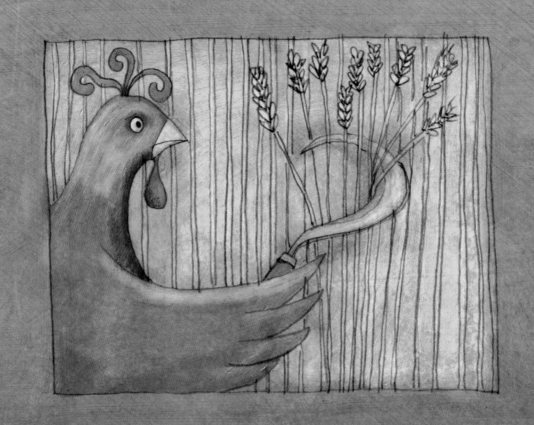

"그럼 나 혼자 잘라야겠군," 암탉이 말했습니다.
암탉은 낫으로 모든 밀들을 잘랐습니다.
그리고 밀들을 묶어 꾸러미를 만들었습니다.

"Then I shall do it all by myself," said Little Red Hen.
She took a sickle and cut down all the wheat. Then she tied it into a bundle.

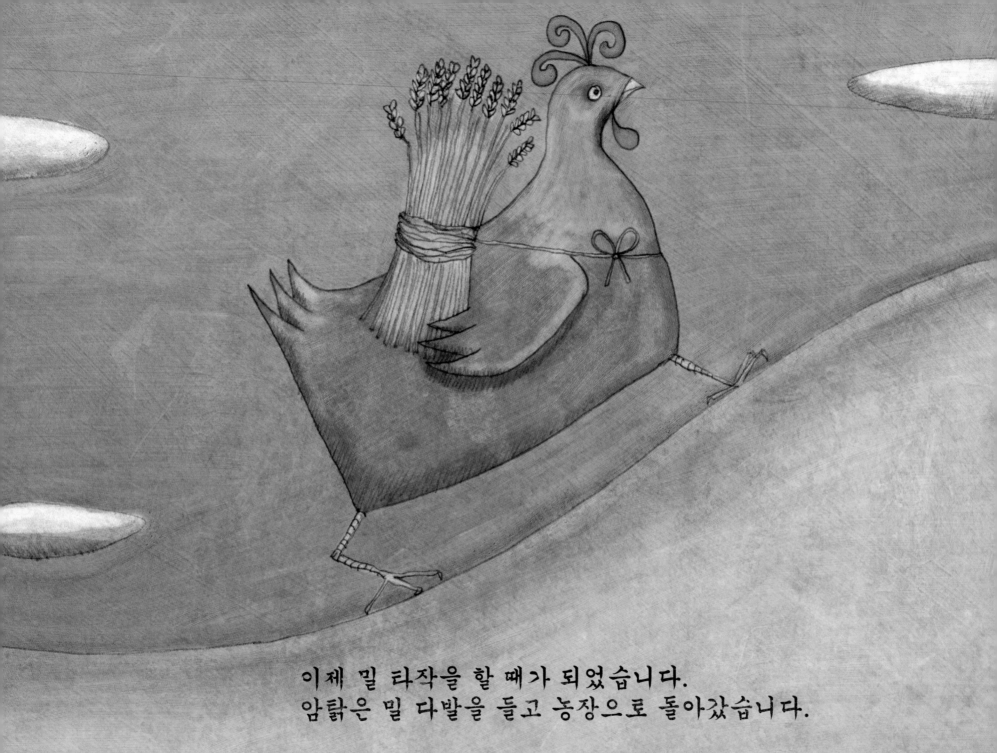

이제 밀 타작을 할 때가 되었습니다.
암탉은 밀 다발을 들고 농장으로 돌아갔습니다.

Now the wheat was ready to thresh.
Little Red Hen carried the bundle of wheat back to the farmyard.

작은 암탉이 동물친구들에게 물었습니다.
"누구 밀 타작을 도와주실래요?"
"난 안돼," 고양이가 말했습니다, "난 너무 바쁘거든."
"난 안돼," 개가 말했습니다, "난 너무 바쁘거든."
"난 안돼," 거위가 말했습니다, "난 너무 바쁘거든."

Little Red Hen called out to the other animals:
"Will anyone help me thresh the wheat?"
"Not I," said the cat, "I'm too busy."
"Not I," said the dog, "I'm too busy."
"Not I," said the goose, "I'm too busy."

"그럼 나 혼자 해야겠군!"
암탉이 말했습니다.

"Then I shall do it all by myself!"
said Little Red Hen.

암탉은 하루종일 밀타작을 했습니다.
밀타작을 끝낸 암탉은 밀들을 손수레에
실었습니다.

She threshed the wheat all day long.
When she had finished she put it into her cart.

이제 밀을 빻아 가루를 만들때가 되었습니다.
그러나 암탉은 너무 지쳐 우리로 들어가 금새 잠이
들어 버렸습니다.

Now the wheat was ready to grind into flour. But Little Red Hen was
very tired so she went to the the barn where she soon fell fast asleep.

다음날 아침 암탉이 동물친구들에게 물었습니다.
"누구 밀 가는 일을 도와주실래요?"
"난 안돼," 고양이가 말했습니다, "난 너무 바쁘거든."
"난 안돼," 개가 말했습니다, "난 너무 바쁘거든."
"난 안돼," 거위가 말했습니다, "난 너무 바쁘거든."

The next morning Little Red Hen called out to the other animals:
"Will anyone help me take the wheat to the mill?"
"Not I," said the cat, "I'm too busy."
"Not I," said the dog, "I'm too busy."
"Not I," said the goose, "I'm too busy."

"그럼 나 혼자 해야겠군!" 암탉이 말했습니다.
암탉은 손수레 가득한 밀을 끌고 방앗간으로 갔습니다.

"Then I shall go all by myself!" said Little Red Hen.
She pulled her cart full of wheat and wheeled it all the way to the mill.

방앗간 주인은 밀을 빻아 가루를 만들었습니다.
이제 빵을 만들때가 되었습니다.

The miller took the wheat and ground it into flour.
Now it was ready to make a loaf of bread.

암탉이 동물친구들에게 물었습니다.
"누구 빵 굽는일 도와주실래요?"
"난 안돼," 고양이가 말했습니다, "난 너무 바쁘거든."
"난 안돼," 개가 말했습니다, "난 너무 바쁘거든."
"난 안돼," 거위가 말했습니다, "난 너무 바쁘거든."

Little Red Hen called out to the other animals:
"Will anyone help me take this flour to the baker?"
"Not I," said the cat, "I'm too busy."
"Not I," said the dog, "I'm too busy."
"Not I," said the goose, "I'm too busy."

"그럼 나 혼자 해야겠군!" 암탉이 말했습니다.
암탉은 무거운 밀가루 자루를 메고 빵집으로 향했습니다.

"Then I shall go all by myself!" said Little Red Hen.
She took the heavy sack of flour all the way to the bakery.

빵집주인은 밀가루에 이스트, 물, 설탕, 소금을 섞었습니다.
빵집주인은 가루반죽을 오븐에 넣고 굽기 시작했습니다.
빵이 구워지자 주인은 암탉에게 빵을 주었습니다.

The baker took the flour and added some yeast, water, sugar and salt.
He put the dough in the oven and baked it.
When the bread was ready he gave it to Little Red Hen.

암탉은 막 구운 빵을 들고 농장으로 돌아왔습니다.

Little Red Hen carried the freshly baked
bread all the way back to the farmyard.

암탉이 동물친구들에게 물었습니다.
"누구 나와 같이 이 맛있는 빵을 먹을래요?"

Little Red Hen called out to the other animals:
"Will anyone help me eat this tasty fresh bread?"

"내가 먹어줄께," 개가 말했습니다,
"난 바쁘지 않거든."

"I will," said the dog, "I'm not busy."

"내가 먹어 줄께," 거위가 말했습니다,
"난 바쁘지 않거든."

"I will," said the goose, "I'm not busy."

"내가 먹어 줄께," 고양이가 말했습니다,
"난 바쁘지않거든."

"I will," said the cat, "I'm not busy."

"오 그래요, 내가 다시 생각 좀 해볼께요!"
암탉이 말했습니다.

"Oh I'll have to think about that!"
said Little Red Hen.

암탉이 방앗간주인과 빵집주인을 초대해 맛있는 빵을 먹고
있을 때 다른 동물친구들은 부러워 쳐다만 보았습니다.

The Little Red Hen invited the miller and the baker to share her
delicious bread while the three other animals all looked on.

key words

little	작은	clouds	구름
red	빨간	rain	비
hen	암탉	sun	태양
farmyard	농지	ripe	익은
farm	농장	plant	심다
goose	거위	cut	자르다
dog	개	sickle	낫
cat	고양이	bundle	꾸러미
wheat	밀	thresh	타작하다
busy	바쁜	grind	갈다

주단

flour	밀가루	tasty	맛좋은
the mill	방앗간	fresh	갓만들어진
miller	방앗간 주인	delicious	맛있는
ground	땅	all	모두, 모든
bread	빵	she	그녀
baker	빵을 굽는 사람	he	그
yeast	누룩		
water	물		
sugar	설탕		
salt	소금		

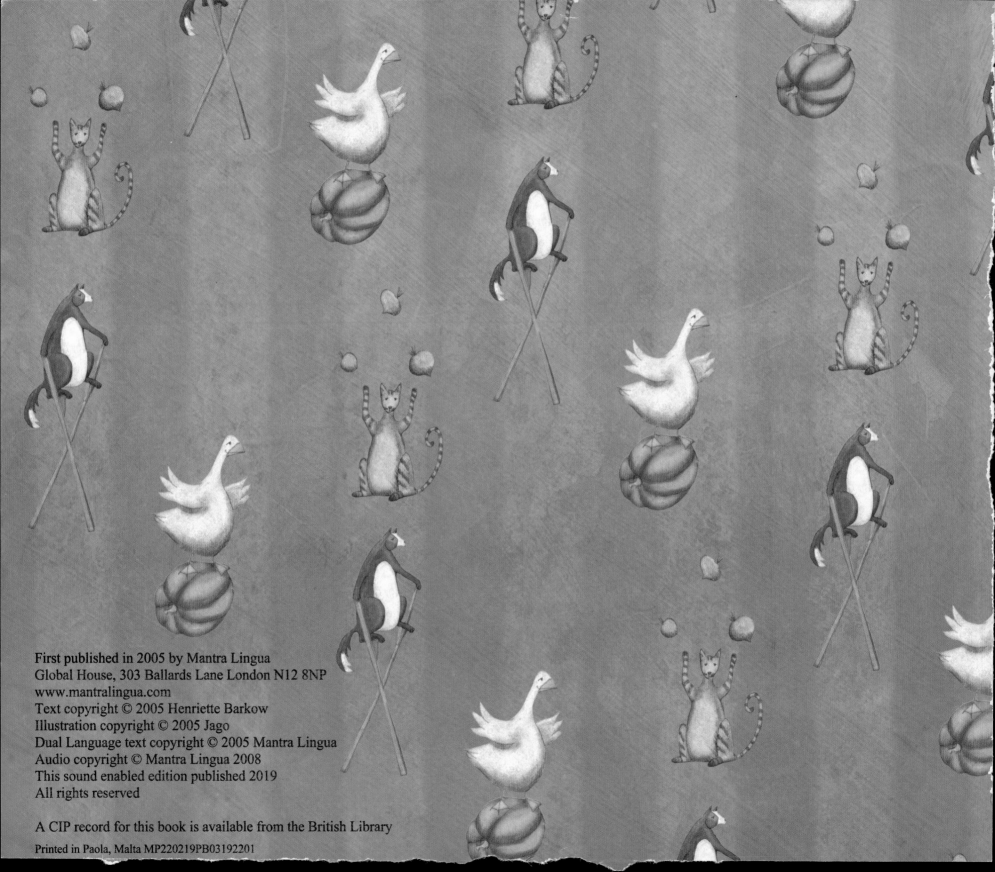

First published in 2005 by Mantra Lingua
Global House, 303 Ballards Lane London N12 8NP
www.mantralingua.com
Text copyright © 2005 Henriette Barkow
Illustration copyright © 2005 Jago
Dual Language text copyright © 2005 Mantra Lingua
Audio copyright © Mantra Lingua 2008
This sound enabled edition published 2019

A CIP record for this book is available from the British Library

Printed in Paola, Malta MP220219PB03192201